# Hairy Maclary, SIT

## Lynley Dodd

Spindlewood

Something was happening
down in the Park;
such a yap
could be heard,
such a blusterous bark.
A fidget of dogs
lined up on the grass
for the Kennel Club's
Special
Obedience
Class.

Hairy Maclary
felt breezily bad,
jittery, skittery,
mischievous,
mad.
The leader said
'SIT!'
but he wouldn't obey.
The other dogs sat
but he scampered
away.

Galloping here,
galloping there,
rollicking,
frolicking,
EVERYWHERE.

'DOWN!'
called the leader,
so tangled in knots
that
off in a hurry
sped Bottomley Potts.

Galloping here,
galloping there,
rollicking,
frolicking,
EVERYWHERE.

'HEEL!'
cried the leader
but
skipping away
to follow the others
went Muffin McLay.

Galloping here,
galloping there,
rollicking,
frolicking,
EVERYWHERE.

'STAY!'
roared the leader,
husky and hoarse,
but
out of his clutches
slipped Hercules Morse.

Galloping here,
galloping there,
rollicking,
frolicking,
EVERYWHERE.

'COME!'
howled the leader
but
looking for fun
were Bitzer Maloney
and Schnitzel von Krumm.

Galloping here,
galloping there,
rollicking,
frolicking,
EVERYWHERE.

'WAIT!'
yelled the leader
but
capering free
went Custard
and Noodle
and Barnacle B.

Galloping here,
galloping there,
rollicking,
frolicking,
EVERYWHERE.

They raced round the fountain,
they chased through the trees,
they barged over gardens
and scattered the leaves.
They hurtled past sheds
and the bandstand beyond;
they rushed through a hedge
and
went …